AF228913

Freshwater Fish

Catfish

Leo Statts

Launch!
An Imprint of Abdo Zoom
abdopublishing.com

abdopublishing.com

Published by Abdo Zoom, a division of ABDO, PO Box 398166, Minneapolis, Minnesota 55439.
Copyright © 2019 by Abdo Consulting Group, Inc. International copyrights reserved in all countries.
No part of this book may be reproduced in any form without written permission from the publisher.
Launch!™ is a trademark and logo of Abdo Zoom.

Printed in the United States of America, North Mankato, Minnesota.

052018
092018

THIS BOOK CONTAINS
RECYCLED MATERIALS

Photo Credits: Alamy, iStock, Minden Pictures, ©John C. Lewis p.19 / SeaPics.com, Shutterstock

Production Contributors: Kenny Abdo, Jennie Forsberg, Grace Hansen, John Hansen

Design Contributors: Dorothy Toth, Neil Klinepier

Library of Congress Control Number: 2017960620

Publisher's Cataloging-in-Publication Data

Names: Statts, Leo, author.

Title: Catfish / by Leo Statts.

Description: Minneapolis, Minnesota : Abdo Zoom, 2019. | Series: Freshwater fish |
    Includes online resources and index.

Identifiers: ISBN 9781532122880 (lib.bdg.) | ISBN 9781532123863 (ebook) |
    ISBN 9781532124358 (Read-to-me ebook)

Subjects: LCSH: Catfishes--Juvenile literature. | Freshwater fishes--Juvenile literature. |
    Catfishes--Behavior--Juvenile literature. | Fishes--Juvenile literature.

Classification: DDC 597.0976--dc23

Table of Contents

4

Many **species** can be found in shallow, flowing water around the world.

Body

Catfish can be many different sizes and colors. They have flat heads. Their mouths are big.

Catfish are known for their **barbels**. The barbels help catfish decide what food is good to eat.

Catfish have eight fins.
They have skin or bony
plates, instead of scales.

Habitat

Catfish can live in fresh water or salt water. **Freshwater** fish live in rivers, ponds, and lakes.

They sink to the bottom of the water they live in. Catfish hide in weeds or under large rocks.

Food
Catfish are carnivores.

They eat insects, frogs, and other fish. Catfish swim along the bottom of their fresh water **habitat** looking for their next meal.

They dig through mud and
sand to find food.

Life Cycle

Some catfish can live
as long as 20 years.

Catfish make a **nest** for their eggs in warmer water. The eggs **hatch** within 10 days.

Average Length

A micro catfish is smaller than a baseball.

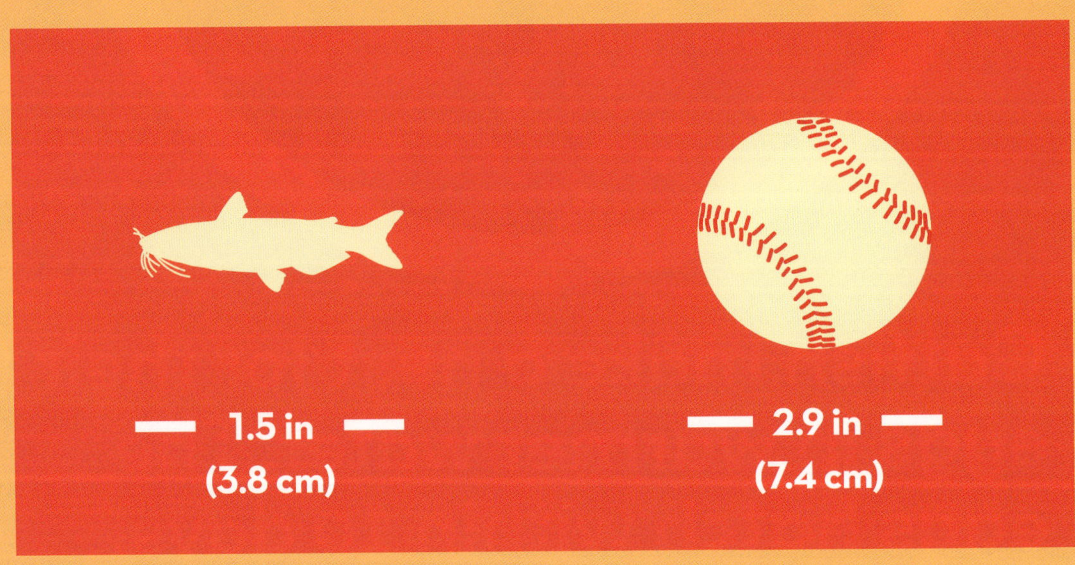

Average Length

A Mekong giant catfish is slightly longer than a sofa.

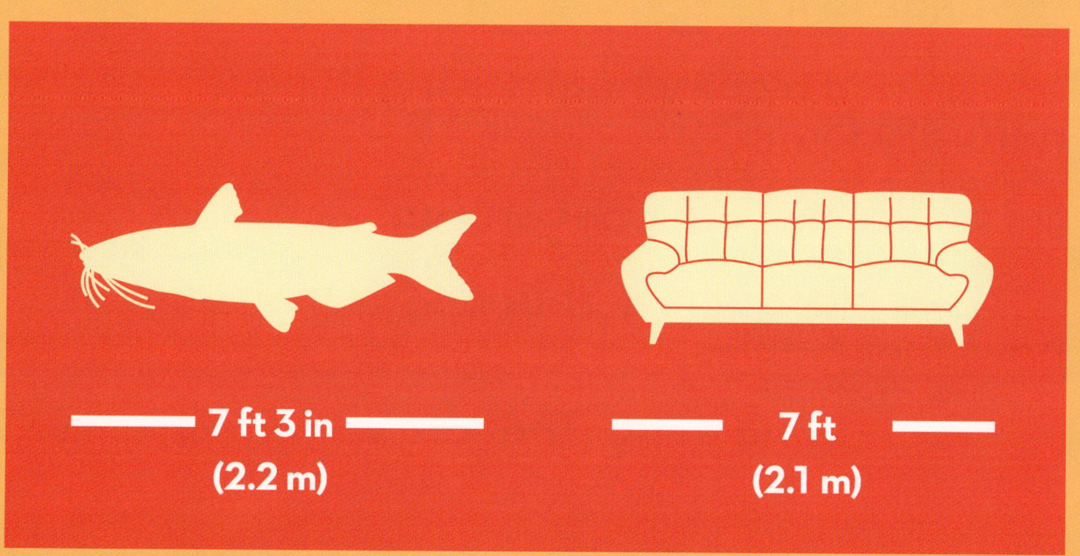

Glossary

barbels – whisker-like organs found near the mouths of catfish that are used to find food.

carnivore – an animal that eats meat.

fin – a body part of a water animal that is shaped like a blade or fan.

freshwater – able to live in water that does not have salt in it.

habitat – a place where a living thing is naturally found.

hatch – to be born from an egg.

nest – a place where animals lay their eggs or have their babies.

species – living things that are very much alike.

Online Resources

For more information on catfish, please visit **abdobooklinks.com**

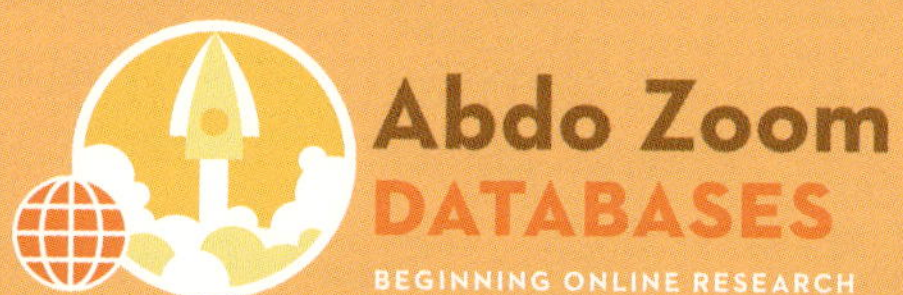

Learn even more with the Abdo Zoom Animals database. Visit **abdozoom.com** today!

Index